A SQUIRMY, WORMY SURPRISE

Read the rest of the books in the
FRIENDSHIP GARDEN
series:

the FRIENDSHIP garden

A SQUIRMY, WORMY SURPRISE

by Jenny Meyerhoff
illustrated by Éva Chatelain

ALADDIN

New York   London   Toronto   Sydney   New Delhi

ALADDIN

An imprint of Simon & Schuster Children's Publishing Division
1230 Avenue of the Americas, New York, New York 10020
First Aladdin paperback edition September 2017
Text copyright © 2017 by Simon & Schuster, Inc.
Illustrations copyright © 2017 by Éva Chatelain
Also available in an Aladdin hardcover edition.
All rights reserved, including the right of reproduction in whole or in part in any form.
ALADDIN and related logo are registered trademarks of Simon & Schuster, Inc.
For information about special discounts for bulk purchases, please contact Simon & Schuster Special Sales at 1-866-506-1949 or business@simonandschuster.com.
The Simon & Schuster Speakers Bureau can bring authors to your live event. For more information or to book an event contact the Simon & Schuster Speakers Bureau at 1-866-248-3049 or visit our website at www.simonspeakers.com.
Book designed by Laura Lyn DiSiena
The text of this book was set in Century Expanded LT Std.
Manufactured in the United States of America 0817 OFF
10 9 8 7 6 5 4 3 2 1
Library of Congress Control Number 2017931902
ISBN 978-1-4814-7055-1 (hc)
ISBN 978-1-4814-7054-4 (pbk)
ISBN 978-1-4814-7056-8 (eBook)

For bookworms everywhere

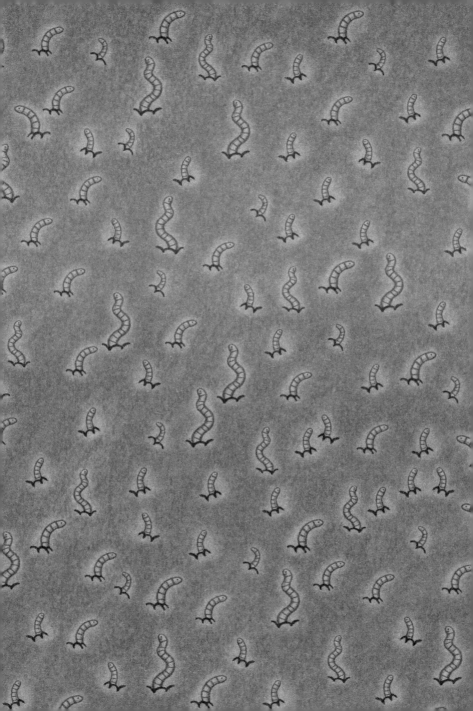

CONTENTS

THE FUN FORECAST

The wheels of Anna's green bicycle bumped over the sidewalk as she rode to Sullivan Magnet School. It wasn't the first day of fourth grade—school didn't start for two more days—but Anna's stomach was still filled with butterflies. Today, class lists would be posted on the front windows of Anna's school. Class list day didn't have an actual name, but

Anna nicknamed it the Fun Forecast. Just like the weather report told Anna whether a day would be sunny or rainy, the class list would tell her whether fourth grade would feel fun and friendly or lost and lonely.

Anna pedaled faster, even though her younger brother, Collin, called from behind her, "Anna, wait up! I can't ride that fast."

Anna didn't want to wait. She needed to find out if Kaya and Reed were in her class. Last year Anna moved to Chicago from upstate New York, and she'd had to make all new friends. It was hard at first, but third grade in Mr. Hoffman's class turned out to be the best year of school ever. Mr. Hoffman helped her start a school garden club, the Friendship Garden, and being in the Friendship Garden helped her find her friends. She didn't want to start all over again in a class where she didn't know anyone.

"Anna Banana!" Anna's father called out. Ever since they moved to Chicago, Anna's dad was the parent who stayed home and took care of Anna and her brother. Anna's mother was a chef at a fancy restaurant.

"Stop at the corner," he added. "We'll all cross the street together."

Anna squeezed the brakes on her handlebars and stopped. Then she watched as Collin rode his bike the rest of the way up the block while her father walked beside him. Why were they so S-L-O-W?

Across the street, the front yard of the school was filled with students and grownups, chatting, laughing, and running around. Closer to the school, a crowd of people blocked the windows. Everyone was trying to get a peek at the lists.

Finally Anna's father and Collin reached the corner, and when the light turned green, they all crossed the street. Anna parked her bike at the bike rack and raced toward the lists. But before she was halfway there, Kaya, her best friend in the whole world, burst from the crowd and zoomed toward her.

"We! Are! In! The! Same! Class!" Kaya shouted, pumping her fists in the air with each word. "And Reed and Bailey too."

Anna grabbed both of Kaya's hands. It was too good to be true: *all* of her new friends in the same class. "Are you sure?"

Kaya nodded. "Come on, I'll show you."

Kaya grabbed Anna's hand and pulled her into the group of people waiting to see the lists. They wove their way through elbows and legs until they were right up at the front.

"There," Kaya said, pointing. "Look!"

Anna looked at the list. At the top it said:

Fourth Grade

Room 13

Miss Lopez

Anna glanced down the list, and she saw her own name, plus Kaya's, Reed's, and Bailey's, but she didn't study the list the way she thought she would. Her eyes bounced right back up to the top of the paper.

Fourth Grade

Room 13

Miss Lopez

Anna grabbed the edge of her T-shirt with her thumb and pointer finger and began to twist the fabric back and forth. She blinked her eyes a couple of times.

"Aren't you excited?" Kaya said, squeezing Anna's arm. "We're all together!"

Anna nodded. She was excited to be in a class with her friends, only she had forgotten something important. Well, she didn't forget exactly. Anna *knew* that Mr. Hoffman wouldn't be her teacher this year. He was a third-grade teacher. But Anna had forgotten to remember that fourth grade would come with a *brand-new* teacher.

Anna had loved Mr. Hoffman more than any other teacher she had ever had before. They had so many things in common. Mr. Hoffman loved vegetable gardening just as much as Anna did. Every day he wore a bow tie with an interesting pattern, and every day Anna wore tights or socks with an interesting pattern. He was silly and funny and liked to host class parties.

The only thing Anna knew about Miss Lopez was that she was the strictest teacher at Sullivan School. One time, Anna had been humming to herself in the hallway, and Miss Lopez had stuck her head out of her classroom door and whisper-yelled, "Shh! Students are taking a test!" Anna's cheeks burned just thinking about it.

Anna wrapped her arms around the hard knot in her belly as she followed Kaya back out of the crowd. They went and stood near a patch of weeds by the side of the school. "We have *Miss Lopez*," Anna said to Kaya. "I heard she doesn't let kids go to the bathroom."

Kaya nodded. "Only at lunch and recess. And I heard her favorite word is *¡Silencio!* But my cousin Vera was in her class a few years ago, and she said Miss Lopez is actually really nice. You just have to give her a chance."

"At least we're together," Anna said, hugging Kaya, but she wished she didn't have to get used to a new teacher.

Anna sighed. Maybe fourth grade wouldn't be so bad. After all, she had her friends, and she still had the Friendship Garden with Mr. Hoffman. Anna looked up at the pale-blue sky dotted with fluffy white clouds and shielded her eyes from the too-bright sun. All in all, she'd say the forecast for fourth grade was sunny with a slight chance of rain.

CLOUDY WITH A CHANCE OF WORMS

On the first day of fourth grade Anna wore her favorite rainbow tights to school. They made her legs hot and itchy as she rode her bike down the sidewalk, but they were lucky tights, and Anna thought fourth grade in Room 13 with Miss Lopez might need a little extra luck.

Anna and Collin parked their bikes at the bike rack, then Anna said good-bye to her father and Collin and walked over to where the fourth-grade classroom numbers were painted on the blacktop. It was hard to see the numbers since so many kids were already standing in line, but finally she was sure she was at number 13. She looked to the head of the line, and there was Mr. Hoffman! Anna couldn't understand why he was standing with the fourth graders. Unless . . .

Maybe he wanted to be her teacher again, so he switched classes!

Anna raced up to the front of the line, her almost-empty backpack bouncing against her shoulders.

"Mr. Hoffman!" she shouted, throwing her arms around him in a big hug. "I'm so glad you

are my teacher again. I was worried school wouldn't be any fun this year, but now I know it will be super extra amazing!"

Mr. Hoffman patted Anna's shoulder. He was wearing a rainbow bow tie! They were totally T-W-I-N-S!

"I'm happy to see you, too," he said, but his voice sounded a little strange. He made an "Oops!" face at the person standing next to him. Anna followed his gaze and saw he was making the face at Miss Lopez. She had been hard to notice before, because she was barely taller than most of the fourth graders.

Anna shook her head in confusion. What was Miss Lopez doing here?

Mr. Hoffman cleared his throat. "I'm pretty sure you are in Miss Lopez's class this year. I'll be teaching fourth grade in Room 14, though, so I'm sure we'll still see a lot of each other."

Anna couldn't believe her ears. Mr. Hoffman was teaching fourth grade, only he wasn't her teacher. She still had Miss Lopez. And now Miss Lopez knew that Anna thought school wouldn't be any fun.

"Uh, hi," Anna said, turning to Miss Lopez as her face burned with embarrassment. "I'm Anna Fincher."

"I know who you are," Miss Lopez said with a funny expression on her face. She straightened her plain black skirt. "I remember you from last year," Miss Lopez added.

Anna gulped. The bell rang.

"You'd better go get in line,"
Miss Lopez said. Anna glanced
around and saw Kaya, Bailey,
and Reed waving her over to
the middle of the line. But Miss
Lopez pointed at the very end
of the line. "No budging," she
said. Anna bit her lip. Did Miss
Lopez think she was a budger?

Anna trudged toward the
end of the line, giving her friends a small wave
as she passed. From the very back of the line
she could barely see Miss Lopez, but it was
easy to see Mr. Hoffman. He took a few steps
to the side, so he was standing in front of his
own class. "All right, Room 14, who's ready for
the best fourth grade year ever?"

All the students in Mr. Hoffman's line cheered. Miss Lopez just stood, watching Mr. Hoffman, with both hands clasped behind her back.

"I've heard you guys are rock-star students, so I want to see you rock out as we walk inside." Mr. Hoffman pretended to play an electric guitar. "Silently, of course," he added as he began walking, playing air guitar. Anna wanted to switch lines and follow his class inside, but he'd only send her back.

She turned to Miss Lopez, wondering how *her* class would walk inside.

"Room 13 students, please follow me." Keeping her hands tucked behind her back, Miss Lopez spun around and walked into school with the plainest, most boring walk in the world.

When they reached the fourth-grade hallway, Anna noticed that one side of the

hall, Mr. Hoffman's side, had big sparkly stars in every color of the rainbow posted all over the wall. Each star had a student's name and school picture in the center of it. Above the stars was a banner that said:

FOURTH-GRADE ROCK STARS

LEARNING IS OUR JAM!

As Anna walked past Miss Lopez's plain, undecorated side of the hallway, she twisted her head to get a little peek inside Mr. Hoffman's room. Inflatable electric guitars hung from the ceiling.

"Welcome to Room 13," Miss Lopez said, pausing outside the door to their classroom. "Please find your cubby at the back of the room and put your things away. Everything must be kept neatly on your hook or shelf. If I find items on the floor, I will send them straight to lost and found. Once your things are put away, please find your desk. Silently."

When Anna reached the doorway, she saw that Miss Lopez had decorated it with—eew!— W-O-R-M-S! The blue door was covered with photographs of slimy red earthworms, each with a student's head attached at one end. The top of the door said:

FOURTH-GRADE BOOKWORMS

Anna took a deep breath. Worms were squirmy and squishy and awful. Every time her spade dug one up in the garden, her stomach quivered with disgust. Her lucky tights hadn't been lucky at all. Suddenly, fourth grade felt like it was overcast with a sky full of the darkest clouds ever!

CHAPTER 3

WITHOUT THE FOGGIEST IDEA

Anna paused in the doorway of Room 13.

She didn't want to go inside.

"Anna?" Miss Lopez raised her eyebrows at Anna. "Is there a problem?"

Anna folded her arms across her chest and shook her head. "No." Anna tried to walk normally into her classroom, but she might have accidentally stomped a little bit. She was about to let out a big sigh, when she stopped and looked around the room.

The bottom half of every wall was covered in spotty brown paper that looked like dirt. Above it was a section of green paper cut in a zigzag along the top so it looked like grass, and above that was blue paper for the sky. Anna almost felt like she was underground, planted in a garden. Right where the brown paper met the green paper, white paper roots sprouted in all directions, and in between the roots were picture of bugs and—ugh!—worms. Lots and lots of worms.

It would have been super C-O-O-L, if it wasn't for all the worms.

"Once you've taken your seats," Miss Lopez began, "please fill out the questionnaires on your desks. I'd like to learn all about you. I'm guessing you'd like to learn about me, too, so I've put my own answers up on the whiteboard."

Anna wanted to keep staring at the decorations, but she quickly found her cubby and put her things away. Then she found her desk—next to Reed!—and looked at the questionnaire and Miss Lopez's answers.

What is your name?

Lara Elena Lopez

How old are you?

29

What is your favorite color?

Green

What is your favorite animal?

Worms!

Anna almost snorted when she read that. Of course that was Miss Lopez's favorite animal. Anna had never met anyone whose favorite animal was *worms*. Not even her brother, Collin, and he loved bugs.

She quickly wrote down her own answers. For favorite color she wrote *Rainbow,* and for favorite animal she wrote *Honeybees.* They had become Anna's favorite over the summer when she learned how important they were for growing fruits and vegetables. Then she turned back to Miss Lopez's list.

What is your favorite book?

Esperanza Rising

What is your fourth-favorite book?

Huh? Anna scratched her head. What kind of question was that? Why wasn't Miss Lopez asking about her second-favorite book, or her third-favorite book? Who even had a fourth-favorite book? Well, Miss Lopez, obviously. It was *Diary of a Worm*. Anna snorted again, then she wrote *The Secret Garden*. Her mother had read it to her over the summer.

If you were stranded on the top of the school and could bring only one thing with you, what would it be?

The questions kept getting stranger and stranger. How could anyone get stranded on top of the school? Students weren't even allowed up there! Maybe it was a trick question, and Miss Lopez was trying to find out who might break the rules. But Miss Lopez had written *My yo-yo*. Anna could not imagine Miss Lopez with a yo-yo.

Just then Anna thought of an answer. She

could bring an apiary, because a roof was the perfect place to keep beehives. Or maybe some dirt, because a rooftop could also be a good site for a garden. But she didn't want Miss Lopez to think she was a rule breaker, so instead she wrote, *I would never climb on the roof without permission, but if I did get stuck there, I would bring a ladder so I could climb down safely.*

The next question was the strangest of all.

Define _____.

(I'm not answering this one. I'd like to see what you think.)

Anna bit her lip. Miss Lopez wasn't just strict, she was W-E-I-R-D. A bunch of kids raised their hands. Anna bet she knew exactly what they wanted to ask: *How do you answer a question that isn't even a question?* or maybe *Define what?*

Miss Lopez wouldn't call on anyone. "There are no right or wrong answers," she said. "Please fill out the questionnaire any way you choose."

Anna didn't know what she was choosing between, but Reed was busy writing, his pencil scribbling enthusiastically. That was strange. Last year Reed was the last kid in the class to start working. He usually bounced around in his chair or squeezed his colorful squeezy balls for a long time before he got busy.

Anna leaned over in her seat a tiny bit. She wasn't going to copy, she just wanted a tiny peek at what Reed was writing so she would know how to answer the question, but his arm was blocking her view. Anna scooted her chair to the side.

"Hey," Reed said suddenly, turning to look at Anna with a confused expression on his face. "What are you doing?" Anna felt everyone's eyes in the entire classroom turn to look at her. Her neck grew warm and itchy, and Miss Lopez said, "I'd like everyone to keep their eyes on their own papers, please. I want *your* answers, not your neighbors'."

Miss Lopez spoke as if she was addressing the entire class, but she was looking only at Anna the entire time. Great! Now Miss Lopez thought she was a cheater. Anna's nose started to get stuffy and her eyes felt hot and wet.

Anna stared at the question and tried to think of an answer. Nothing came to her mind. Her brain was filled with fog. What if Anna couldn't think of any answers for the whole entire school year? What if Miss Lopez asked only crazy questions that had no real answers? The fog in Anna's mind kept getting thicker and thicker. She felt like she was disappearing into a bleary, blurry cloud. Worst of all, she didn't have the foggiest idea how to finish her questionnaire.

What is your name?
How old are you?
What is your favorite color?
What is your favorite animal?

A PERSONAL, PRIVATE RAIN CLOUD

Miss Lopez stood at the front of the room, staring at everyone while they worked on their questionnaires. But Anna felt like Miss Lopez was staring at her the most. It made the skin on the back of her neck crawl.

"Please bring your questionnaires to my in-box when you are finished." Miss Lopez pointed to a red tray on her desk. "This is where you will turn in all your work. If it is not in my in-box, it doesn't count as being turned in."

Anna gulped. Reed hopped up and turned in his paper. Miss Lopez glanced at his work, then smiled at him. "I love when students aren't afraid of their imaginations. I think we're going to have fun together this year."

"Me too," said Reed. He practically skipped back to his seat. Anna's final question was still blank, and little beads of sweat were forming all along the edge of her forehead.

One by one the other students in her class stood up and handed in their questionnaires as well. Anna leaned over and whispered to Reed, "I wasn't trying to copy you. I was just trying to figure out how to answer the question."

"What do you mean?" Reed whispered back. "There's no trick—you just answer it."

"But I'm not even sure what the question is!" Anna shook her head. "This is impossible."

"*Silencio, por favor*," Miss Lopez said, and Anna felt her teacher's eyes staring right at her. "There is no reason to be talking right now. You have one more minute to finish your questionnaires, then I'll need everyone to turn them in, even if they are incomplete."

Anna's heart began to race. She needed to answer that last question, and fast. Anna decided she'd pick the first word she thought of and fill in the blank.

The first word that came to her mind was *compost*. Just that morning her father told her that there was a problem with the Friendship Garden's compost bin: It smelled like rotten eggs! S-T-I-N-K-Y! He was going to come to the Friendship Garden the next afternoon and help Maria and Mr. Hoffman handle the problem.

Anna wrote the word *compost* on the line and then wrote a definition: a mix of old food, brown paper, and water that turns into soil (after a loooooong time).

When she was finished, Anna walked up to Miss Lopez's desk to turn in her paper. There were a couple of kids ahead of her, so she waited.

First Kaya turned in her paper, and Miss Lopez said, "A painter! I was wondering who my class artist would be." Anna watched as Kaya beamed up at their teacher.

Then a boy with curly hair turned in his paper, and Miss Lopez said, "Ho-ho! A jokester! I bet you'll keep me on my toes." The boy laughed as if Miss Lopez had made a joke, then he went back to his seat.

Anna was next. She stepped forward and with a shaking hand gave her paper to Miss Lopez. She wondered what her teacher would say. Maybe she would call Anna the class gardener, or a Green Thumb Girl. But Miss Lopez just looked at Anna's paper and said, "Thank you. You may return to your seat now."

Anna's heart sank as she turned around and plodded back to her seat. Miss Lopez probably hated her. Anna's heart stayed sunken all the way through gym, lunch, math, and recess. At the end of the day, even though she was supposed to be writing in her journal, Anna could barely keep her eyes off the clock. Finally, Miss Lopez stood up and told her class to put their notebooks away.

"Okay, class. I'd like to tell you about one of my favorite parts of fourth grade." Miss Lopez began to write a few words on the whiteboard, but Anna didn't read them. She already knew her teacher's favorite part of fourth grade: torturing students.

"Psst, Anna," Reed whispered. Then a little slip of paper landed on her desk. Anna opened it. It read, *What's wrong?*

Anna didn't bother writing back. Miss Lopez already hated her, so it didn't matter if she got in trouble for talking again.

"Miss Lopez really doesn't like me." Anna let her shoulders droop.

Reed gave Anna a sympathetic smile. "My brother had Miss Lopez, and he told me that if she likes you you're golden, but if she doesn't she makes you miserable."

"I knew it," Anna said, frowning.

"Yeah, but he also told me that Miss Lopez didn't like him at first, *until* he volunteered to keep track of all her playground equipment, because it kept going missing. Then she liked him a lot and he had a great year. So all you have to do is figure out how to make her like you."

Anna knew Reed was just trying to be helpful, so she gave him a trembly smile. But she couldn't see any way to get Miss Lopez to like her. Anna turned back to Miss Lopez and tried to pay attention. She'd missed almost everything her teacher had been explaining about their new assignment.

"So, do any of you have any questions about your first Curiosity Quest?" Miss Lopez asked.

"Can we really do any topic we want?" Bailey asked. "Anything in the whole world?"

Miss Lopez smiled. "Yes and no," she said. "I want you to pick something that you feel really curious about, but you need to be able to ask a question about your topic that won't be either too easy or too hard to answer."

"Are you sure we don't have to write a report about it?" another kid asked.

"You can write a report if you want to, but you could also make a movie or write a song. You could paint a picture or give a speech. I want *you* to decide how you will demonstrate what you've learned. You guys are old enough to create your own assignments sometimes."

Just then the bell rang. The first day of fourth grade was officially over!

"Don't forget," Miss Lopez called out as everyone headed to the back of the room to get their things. "I want everyone to bring in a topic for their first Curiosity Quest on Monday."

Anna sighed. She bet it wouldn't even matter what she picked. Miss Lopez wouldn't like her topic, just because it was hers. Everyone else in the class seemed happy and cheerful. It was like they were all standing out in the sunshine, and Anna had her own personal, private thunderstorm bursting over her head. And Anna didn't have an umbrella.

RAIN, RAIN, GO AWAY

The next day, when the bell rang after school, Anna took a deep breath. She let it out in a giant sigh. She'd made it through another day! Even though Anna's first two days of fourth grade had been overcast, she didn't want to let it ruin her afternoon. After all, not only was it Friday—the beginning of the weekend—it was also the first meeting of the Friendship Garden Club. Anna, Kaya, Bailey, and Reed walked to the flagpole in the front of the school. That's where Mr. Hoffman met all the kids in the club. Then, together, they would walk a few blocks to the Shoots and Leaves Community Garden.

Anna was surprised to see how many kids were standing by the flagpole. Last year there had been about eight kids in the Friendship Garden, but this year it looked to be more like twenty! Anna knew it was a good thing that their club had become more popular, but she wondered if Mr. Hoffman would have any time for her.

Just then, Mr. Hoffman came walking out of the front door of school, right toward the flagpole.

"Hi, Mr. Hoffman!" Anna called out as he

44

reached the group. She tried to get closer to him so she could walk next to him, but a couple of other kids beat her to it.

"Let's get right to the garden," Mr. Hoffman said. "We've got a lot of stuff to talk about on our first day."

Mr. Hoffman started walking, and the group followed along. Kaya's abuela, Daisy, was at the back of the pack. "*¡Hola, niños!*" she called out to them.

Anna and her friends all waved to her.

"Should we go walk with your grandma?" Anna asked.

Kaya shook her head. "My little cousin Mateo is in kindergarten this year, so he's going to do the Friendship Garden too. I love him, but he's always copying everything I say and jumping on my back for a piggyback ride. I don't feel like carrying him today!"

"Your Curiosity Quest should be about how to get little kids to leave you alone," said Reed as they settled into the middle of the crowd walking to Shoots and Leaves.

Anna laughed. "I want to do a Curiosity Quest about how to get a normal teacher. Can't she give us a real assignment? You know, where she tells us what we have to do?"

Anna expected her friends to laugh, but they just looked at her like she had grown an extra head.

"I think the Curiosity Quest is a cool project," Kaya said. "I'm going to do something about the painter Frida Kahlo. Or maybe about dolphins."

"You could do a painting for your final project!" Bailey said. "I think I want to learn about space travel, like, what does it feel like to be all the way out in space. Plus, I want to make my presentation like a planetarium show."

"Well, I already know what I'm going to do," Reed said. "I want to learn how magic tricks work. And then I'm going to do a magic show. I can't believe we actually get to learn stuff like this in school!"

"Are you going to do something about gardening, Anna?" Kaya pointed toward the Friendship Garden at the end of the block as the group of students moved closer.

"I guess," Anna said, kicking at a weed sprouting through the cracks of the sidewalk. "But Miss Lopez probably won't like my idea. She hates me."

"I'm sure she doesn't hate you," Bailey said.

"I heard she was super strict, but I think those were just rumors."

"Yeah, she even told me I could listen to music while I do my work as long as nobody else could hear it through my headphones," Reed said. "She might be my favorite teacher ever."

Anna thought Reed was crazy. "What about Mr. Hoffman? *He* was the best teacher ever."

"I like Mr. Hoffman," said Bailey. "But I like Miss Lopez, too. You can like more than one teacher, you know."

Anna shrugged one shoulder. She guessed that was true. She still liked her first-grade teacher, Mrs. Pointer, even though she didn't remember her that well anymore. But she liked Mr. Hoffman the best. Anna looked at Kaya.

"Mr. Hoffman is my favorite teacher *so far*," Kaya said.

Anna folded her arms across her chest and gave Bailey and Reed her "I told you so" face.

"But," Kaya continued, "I only just met Miss Lopez. It's not fair to compare them."

Anna pouted as they walked through the gate of Shoots and Leaves. "It's like she's brain-washed all of you."

"I told you," Reed said. "You just have to figure out a way to make her like you. Then you'll see what we're talking about."

Anna scratched her head as she followed her friends to the back of Shoots and Leaves and the Friendship Garden's plot. It was close to the compost bin; Anna could tell because the whole area smelled like someone had cracked open a million rotten eggs.

"Eeew!" said Reed. "This place stinks."

Anna walked over to her father, who was standing with Maria, the president of Shoots and Leaves, next to the compost bin. It was so smelly Anna had to pinch her nose with her fingers.

"Hi, Dad," she said in a funny pinched-nose voice.

"Hey there, Banana! How was school?"

Anna wrinkled her eyebrows. She was about to tell her father that school with Miss Lopez wasn't all she'd hoped it would be, when a voice interrupted her. It was Mr. Hoffman.

"I want to know too!" he said. "I think Miss Lopez will be the perfect teacher for you. That's why I put you in her class."

Anna just stood with her mouth hanging open, trying to make sense of Mr. Hoffman's words. He *chose* to put her in Miss Lopez's class instead of his own. It didn't make any sense.

"Uh, school was okay," she said, chewing on the inside of her lip. "Miss Lopez let us go to the library to research our Curiosity Quests. We have to make up our own project."

Anna wrinkled her eyebrows to show how strange she thought the idea was, and Maria laughed. "For a girl who's always coming up with imaginative ideas, that sounds perfect! This new teacher really is just right for our Anna."

Mr. Hoffman nodded. "I know! Miss Lopez is going to love her!"

"Everyone loves Anna," Anna's father said, ruffling her hair.

Anna gave them all a weak smile, then slowly backed away. Everyone seemed to think Anna and Miss Lopez should be best friends or something, but they couldn't be more wrong. Anna and Miss Lopez were opposites, like day and night, inside and out-side, sun and rain. And the more everyone told her they should be like two peas in a pod, the more hopeless Anna felt.

Anna went to the corner of the garden

bed and began to pull weeds along with her friends. As she dug her fingers down into the soil, she wondered what would happen when everyone realized Miss Lopez would never like her. Would they stop liking her too? Anna wished she could plant herself in the garden and stay there all year instead of going back to fourth grade.

CHAPTER 6

A TINY BIT OF SUN

Sometimes when Anna needed to figure things out, she talked to her plants at home. But Anna hoped that maybe the gourds in the Friendship Garden would be good listeners too. Her friends were all busy weeding in their own sections of the bed. Anna crossed her fingers that no one would notice.

"Everyone likes Miss Lopez," she leaned

forward and whispered to the biggest bird-house gourd. "And they think I should too. But I can't because *she* doesn't like *me*."

Anna let out a big sigh and pulled a few more weeds. Then she explained her problem to a spotted green gooseneck gourd. "Mr. Hoffman and all the other grown-ups think she is going to love me. But she doesn't."

"What did you say?" Reed asked, leaning closer to Anna.

"Nothing!" Anna pretended to smile, then she lowered her voice as Reed went back to weeding. "He thinks if I can make her like me, I will have a good year. What do you guys think?"

Of course the gourds didn't answer, but whenever Anna talked to plants, somehow the answer came into her head. "So that's settled, then. I will just have to figure out some way to make her like me."

Starting on Monday Anna would make sure that she followed all the rules and did everything Miss Lopez asked. She wouldn't look at anyone's paper or talk in class or hum in the hallway.

On the way home from the Friendship Garden Anna's father told her he wasn't sure they would be able to save the compost. Compost was like Goldilocks. Everything had to be *just right*. It couldn't be too wet or too dry, but the Friendship Garden compost bin had gotten much too wet. The leaf clippings and vegetable scraps were supposed to decompose and turn into soil, but instead they had been putrefy-ing, turning slimy and stinky. Even worse, the smelly heap had started to attract rats.

Anna shuddered. Rats were almost as bad as worms. But she couldn't really concentrate on what her father was saying because she kept thinking about how to get Miss Lopez to like her.

"Dad," Anna asked, "what makes people like each other?"

Anna's father tilted his head to the side as he walked. "Hmm. I guess first of all people like people who are nice and kind."

Anna nodded. That was true. She liked Mr. Hoffman because he was really nice, but she didn't like Miss Lopez because she was mean to Anna.

"Next, I suppose we like people who have

things in common with us. Like how both your mom and I like cooking and playing card games."

That was true too. Anna liked Mr. Hoffman because they had so many things in common, but Anna had nothing in common with Miss Lopez. Unless . . .

That was it! Anna's father had given her a brilliant idea. Anna and Miss Lopez didn't have anything in common as far as Anna could tell, but Miss Lopez didn't know that. And Anna wasn't going to tell her. Anna remembered once learning about a special kind of flower that tricked bees into collecting its pollen by making its petals look like another bee. Anna would do the same thing. She would trick Miss Lopez into liking her by making her teacher think that Anna was another Miss Lopez. Her Curiosity Quest would also be a teacher trap.

As they arrived home, Anna's father added one more thought. "I think last of all, most of us really like other people who are authentic, just being themselves."

"Mmm, hmm," Anna answered as she opened the door, but she wasn't really paying attention. She had a plan, and for the first time all day she felt like maybe a tiny bit of sun was peeking out from behind her dark cloud.

CHAPTER 7

SPLASHING IN PUDDLES

When Anna walked into Room 13 on Monday morning, she felt full of hope. She was wearing a green shirt, with green socks and a green hair ribbon: Miss Lopez's favorite color. Today Anna would make Miss Lopez like her, and fourth grade would be filled with rainbows and sunshine.

During the Pledge of Allegiance, Anna

said the words extra loud and clear. During math, Anna made sure to connect the top of her eights all the way closed instead of leaving them open and messy like she usually did. And when her class walked in the hallway to and from music, Anna kept her hands behind her back and didn't hum a single hum.

When they got back from lunch, Anna was certain it would finally be time to tell Miss Lopez the topic of her Curiosity Quest and make Miss Lopez like her, but instead, Miss Lopez said she wanted to tell them about their first science unit: ecosystems.

"As part of that unit, we are going to transform the weed patch at the side of the school into a butterfly habitat. Then in the spring, hopefully, the butterflies will come live in our habitat when we do our life-cycle unit."

At first, Anna sat politely paying attention just as she'd planned, but halfway through Miss Lopez's talk, Anna felt like her body was filled with jumping beans. She had realized something important. A butterfly habitat was another word for a *garden*. A flower garden! Miss Lopez wanted her class to plant the kinds of flowers that butterflies loved. The garden would be located on the side of the school. Maybe Anna and Miss Lopez did have something in common.

"I will need a couple of students to volunteer to help me during recess the rest of the week. We need to get the weed patch ready to be planted. Would anyone like to help?"

Anna raised her hand so high up she thought it might fly to the ceiling if it wasn't attached. There were a bunch of other kids

with their hands raised, so Anna shifted in her seat and tucked one leg up under her bottom so her hand would be higher than anyone else's hand. She also accidentally made two tiny *mmm* sounds when she was trying to stretch her hand an extra bit more.

"I'm only going to choose people who are

sitting quietly and politely," Miss Lopez said.

Anna put her foot back on the floor, but kept her arm stretched as high as possible.

"There are so many of you! We'll have to take turns. Reed, Parker, and Kaya, you can be my helpers to start." Miss Lopez wrote their names on the board underneath the words *Butterfly Habitat Helpers*. Anna blinked at the board, and her chest felt fuzzy and hollow. She had been certain she was going to get picked. Nobody liked gardening more than Anna did!

But Anna guessed it didn't matter how much you liked gardening, it only mattered how much Miss Lopez liked *you*.

"I will now meet with each student for one minute at my conference table. Please come to the front of the room when I call your name.

Everyone else, please read silently."

Anna pulled her book, *Esperanza Rising,* out of her desk. Reed leaned over and whispered, "Sorry you didn't get picked." But Anna didn't whisper back. She held up her book and started to read, making sure that the cover of the book was facing Miss Lopez.

Anna tried to read, but it was hard because she kept watching Miss Lopez as the other students told her their topics. Sometimes Miss Lopez had a very serious face and nodded a lot. Sometimes she got a big smile on her face and laughed. Twice she wrinkled up her nose and shook her head. Anna felt bad for those kids.

Finally Miss Lopez called her name. "Anna? Would you come tell me about your topic?"

Anna very carefully placed a bookmark in her book, still making sure that Miss Lopez could see the cover. Then she straightened her green hair ribbon and walked to the table at the back of the room.

"Have you thought of a topic?" Miss Lopez asked.

"Yes." Anna nodded. "A really good one: worms!"

Anna waited for Miss Lopez to smile and laugh, or at least to get serious and nod, but Miss Lopez didn't do either of those things. Instead, Miss Lopez's face looked like it was still waiting. "Go on," she said.

"Go on?" asked Anna.

"Yes," said Miss Lopez. "Tell me. What specifically do you want to know about worms?"

Anna thought about Miss Lopez's question.

The truth was, there wasn't anything she *specifically* wanted to know about worms. Worms were gross. The only thing she wanted to know was how to keep them far, far away.

Miss Lopez put down her pencil and tilted her head at Anna. "Do you have a question or a curiosity about worms?"

"I just want to know all the cool things about them," Anna said, trying to smile.

Miss Lopez frowned. Anna didn't get it. Miss Lopez loved worms. They were her favorite animal. Why would she frown at Anna's topic?

"Tell me, Anna, what made you choose worms as your topic?"

Anna shifted uncomfortably in her seat. This wasn't going the way she had imagined at all. She shrugged one shoulder. "I don't know."

Miss Lopez twisted her mouth to the side, like she was thinking hard about something. "Do you remember when I explained the Curiosity Quest? The topic needs to be in the form of a question."

Anna bit her lip. She hadn't been listening too carefully then. She had been thinking about how much Miss Lopez didn't like her.

"Maybe worms aren't the best topic for

you. Maybe there is another subject you'd be more interested in."

"No!" Anna shrank back, startled at how loud she'd been. She continued in a softer voice. "I really like worms."

"I'll tell you what." Miss Lopez flipped her notebook over so that all Anna could see was a blank sheet of paper. "Why don't you take another day or two and think about your topic? Try to come up with a question that you are burning with curiosity to answer."

Anna nodded. Her eyes felt hot and itchy and there was a lump in her throat. She didn't feel like she could answer out loud.

"And if you decide you want to change your topic, that's fine." Now Miss Lopez did give her a serious look, but there was no nodding. "Your should pick something you are fascinated with, okay? Now, go on back to your desk."

Anna slumped back to her desk, then buried her face behind her book. It seemed that no matter what she did, she would never get Miss Lopez to like her. Anna wanted to give up, but then she'd never get to work on the butterfly habitat.

No, Anna would never give up. Maybe this whole year would be rain showers and thunderstorms. But Anna was going to put on her rain boots and splash in the puddles. She'd find a way to like worms, and she'd find a way to get Miss Lopez to like her. Most important, she'd find a way to work in the butterfly habitat, no matter what!

CHAPTER 8

A FRESH NEW DAY

That night after dinner Anna sat at the computer and Googled *What makes worms cool.* She found a lot of articles about keeping worms out of sunlight and about how worms prefer moist, dark, and cool environments. That wasn't the kind of cool she meant!

Anna also found out that there are more than six thousand kinds of worms and that worms breathe through their skin, but those facts made her shiver with the creeps, not with excitement. In fact, the more Anna learned about worms, the more she *didn't* like them. At this rate she'd never get to work in the butterfly habitat.

Later, after she'd brushed her teeth and watered her plants and was all tucked into bed, Anna's father came into her room to say good night.

"Did you finish all your homework?" he asked.

"Sort of," Anna said. She still hadn't come up with a question that fascinated her, but Miss Lopez had said "another day or two," so Anna still had time. "One of the things isn't actually due tomorrow."

Anna's father nodded. "Okay, good. I'm

going to need your help at the Friendship Garden tomorrow."

"With what?" Anna asked. "The stinky compost?"

"Yeah. I think it needs manure and more air. We need some kids to help us turn the pile. Are you up for it?"

Manure? G-R-O-S-S! Anna didn't love the idea of working with that stinky smell, but she knew that compost was the best thing for a garden's soil. "I'm up for it!"

"Great," he said, kissing her forehead. "Sweet dreams."

Anna fell asleep right away, but she didn't remember her dreams.

The next day at recess, Anna sat on the swing at the edge of the playground and watched as

Bailey and the other new helpers got to work in the weed patch with Miss Lopez. Anna hadn't been chosen for a second day in a row! It was so U-N-F-A-I-R!

"There you are," Kaya said, walking over to the swing set. "I've been looking all over the playground for you. Do you want to play four square?"

Anna shook her head. "Did you know that monarch caterpillars are the only caterpillars that can eat milkweed leaves? We should plant a lot of milkweed in our butterfly garden. Butterfly gardens need to have plants that butterflies like and plants that caterpillars like."

"Wow," said Kaya, sitting on the swing next to Anna. "How do you know all that stuff?"

Anna shrugged. "I looked it up." Anna

had gotten bored of her worm research, so she'd switched to butterfly gardens just for a tiny bit.

"You should be over there with them," Kaya said, nodding her head toward the weed patch.

"I know." Anna sighed. The only way that would happen was if she figured out a way to become as interested in worms as she was in butterfly gardens. But Anna just couldn't see

that happening. "Want to have a swinging contest?" she asked Kaya.

"Sure!"

Anna pumped her legs as hard as she could and her swing soared up and up and up. She closed her eyes and imagined a butterfly soaring over the playground looking for a spot to land. If she didn't come up with a question for her Curiosity Quest, that poor butterfly would just have to keep on flying.

That afternoon, as they all walked to the Friendship Garden, Anna was silent as her friends talked about the butterfly habitat. *They* had all gotten turns to help.

"Miss Lopez said the ground was much sandier than she expected," Bailey told her.

"Yeah," said Reed. "She is worried that our

plants and flowers won't take root, and when spring comes around we'll just have a bunch of dead plants."

"She said if we can't figure out a way to improve the soil, we might have to forget about the butterfly habitat project," Kaya said, dragging her feet.

"It's not that hard to get the soil ready for planting," Anna told them. "After you pull the weeds and turn the dirt, all you have to do is add good stuff, like compost."

"But where are we going to get compost?" Reed asked.

"Easy," Anna told him. "We can ask Shoots and Leaves if we can have some of their compost."

When the group reached the gate of Shoots and Leaves, Anna and her friends could smell the stinky compost heap from all the way across the garden.

"P.U.," said Reed. "If we borrow that, our school will stink too. No way!"

Anna and her friends walked over to her father, who handed them shovels. "Are you ready?" he asked. "First we have to fluff up the pile so more air can get to the stuff in the middle, then we need to add manure and shredded leaves. That should help our compost pile."

Anna tried to breathe through her mouth, so she wouldn't have to smell the awful stench.

"Why does compost smell so bad?" Reed asked.

"It doesn't," said Anna's father. "Well, it shouldn't, not if everything is decomposing properly. And if we can get this pile back on track, it'll smell like fresh dirt."

Just then Mr. Hoffman interrupted their digging. "Hi, everyone, I brought you another helper."

Anna turned around, and her heart sank when she saw that the helper was Miss Lopez.

"Miss Lopez wanted some gardening advice, so I suggested she join our meeting today."

"Glad to have you," said Anna's father, handing Miss Lopez a rake. "Right now we're mixing the pile with air while I add in dry materials."

"Miss Lopez," said Kaya. "Once the compost is ready, we can ask Maria if we can use it for the butterfly habitat. It'll make the soil much better."

"Wonderful! When will it be ready?" asked Miss Lopez.

"I'd estimate about seven months," said

Anna's father. "If it works. It'll be longer if we have to start over completely."

Miss Lopez shook her head. "I'm afraid we may have to cancel, then. That's a little too long for us to wait."

Anna felt her spirits droop. So far there had been only one good thing about fourth grade in Room 13, and that had been the chance of working on the butterfly garden. If Miss Lopez canceled, then Anna would have nothing to look forward to.

"Maybe we could figure out a way to make the pile turn into compost faster," Anna suggested.

Anna's father shook his head. "Sorry, honey, but nature can't be rushed."

"Isn't there some other place we can get compost?" Anna asked Miss Lopez. "We can't cancel the butterfly habitat."

Miss Lopez tilted her head and looked at Anna with surprise. "It seems like the butterfly habitat is really important to you."

"It is," Anna told her. "Gardening is one of my favorite things in the world."

"Interesting," said Miss Lopez, rubbing her chin. "That's a pretty unique hobby for a fourth grader. I wonder why you never mentioned your interest before."

Anna wrinkled her eyebrows. She thought she had mentioned it. In her questionnaire she'd said that bees were her favorite animal, and she'd defined *compost*. But Anna could see that it wasn't very clear. She shrugged her shoulders. "I forgot, I guess."

"Have you had any luck coming up with a question for your Curiosity Quest?" Miss Lopez asked. "Because maybe you should—"

"Oh yes!" Anna said before Miss Lopez could finish her sentence. She hadn't really had any luck, but she didn't want to give Miss Lopez a reason to feel disappointed in her. "I have a great question."

"Wonderful," said Miss Lopez. "Do you want to tell it to me right now?"

Anna's stomach dropped like she was on a roller coaster. "Uh, no. It's not one hundred percent finished yet. It'll be better if I tell you tomorrow."

"Okay," said Miss Lopez. "And, if you think of any ideas to help our soil, let me know about that, too."

Anna kept turning and flipping the soil, and even though it smelled stinkier than a pile of dirty diapers, Anna wondered if soon it might smell like a fresh, new day.

CHAPTER 9

SPRINGING INTO SPRING

That night Anna sat down at the computer, determined to find a question about worms, but everything she learned just made her shudder. Anna learned that some people eat worms, that most worms won't really become two worms if you cut them in half (Anna thought that was pretty good news), and that worms have tiny bristles all over their bodies that help them move through the ground. C-R-E-E-P-Y!

But Anna didn't really learn anything that made her want to know more about worms. Anna threw her hands up in the air and shouted to herself, "Worms are the worst!"

Anna's dad poked his head up from the couch, where he had been reading a new cookbook. "Worms are actually pretty important. Why do you think they are the worst?"

"Because I have to think of a question about them for my Curiosity Quest, and I can't think of anything I want to know." Anna folded her arms on the edge of the desk and let her head rest on her hands.

"Well, why did you pick them for your topic?" her father asked. "You must have had some reason."

Anna spoke to the floor. "I picked them because Miss Lopez likes worms, and I want Miss Lopez to like me."

Anna's father didn't answer, but a minute later she felt his hand on her back. "I understand why you want Miss Lopez to like you, but I'm pretty sure she wants you to pick a topic that *you* like, not one that she likes."

Anna sighed. She thought about how interested Miss Lopez had been when she realized that Anna liked gardening. But it was too late. She'd already picked worms, *and* she'd already told Miss Lopez that she had a great question. "I know you're right, but I still have to do this homework. Now it really is due tomorrow."

"I'll tell you what," said her father. "Why don't I go in the kitchen and whip us up a snack while you take a break from worms and look at topics that *you* find fascinating?"

"But, Dad, I already told her I was doing worms."

"Just for fun," he said. "Then I can help you think of a worm question after our snack."

Anna nodded, and her father went into the kitchen. She thought about what questions were most interesting to her right now, and she realized she wanted to know even more about the butterfly habitat. What kind of butterflies prefer each kind of plant? What else do butterflies need besides plants? And most important, what makes the best soil?

Anna learned lots of great things. She learned that different butterflies liked different kinds of flowers, so the butterfly garden would have to have a big variety. She also learned that it's important to include lots of places where butterflies can lay their eggs. But if the soil of the weed patch couldn't be improved, the class wouldn't even get to plant their garden.

Anna's father came back, and he brought her a smoothie.

"How do you feel now?" he asked.

"A little better," she said. "I know I should have done my project about gardening. That's what I'm really interested in. But I don't want to change now. I already told Miss Lopez I had an idea. If only there was some way to combine the topics."

"I think she would understand. But if you really won't change topics . . ."

Anna's dad took a long sip of his smoothie, then squeezed both his eyes shut. "Brain freeze!" When he opened his eyes again, he gave her a strange look. "Maybe there *is* a way to combine them. Have you looked for it yet?"

Anna shook her head. She hadn't looked. Could he be right? Anna quickly put her smoothie to the side and started Googling. She found out that having worms in the soil was a great thing for gardens (which she already knew), even though worms gave her the heebie-jeebies. But when she kept searching, she came across a word she'd never seen before: *vermicomposting.*

Anna sat up straight. Vermicomposting was making compost with worms. It was easy to do, much faster than regular composting, and if she taught all the fourth graders how to do it, it would be the perfect way to help the soil in the butterfly habitat.

Anna finally had her question: How do you make compost with worms? And her project: making the compost. She couldn't wait to get to school the next day and tell Miss Lopez. Who knew that slimy, disgusting worms actually had something interesting about them after all? It was a squirmy, wormy surprise.

* * *

The next day Anna couldn't wait to tell Miss Lopez about her discovery. She raced right over to where her teacher stood on the yellow number 13.

"Miss Lopez!" she called out. "Not only did I think of a question for my Curiosity Quest, but I think it's going to help our butterfly habitat too!"

Miss Lopez smiled and nodded. "You seem really excited about your idea," she said. "I can't wait to hear what it is."

"It's *How can worms help us make compost?*" Anna told Miss Lopez everything she had learned about worms and soil. "Some people don't even call it compost," she gushed. Anna was so excited to tell Miss Lopez

everything, her words were tumbling out of her.

Miss Lopez laughed. "I thought I knew everything about worms, but you just taught me something new. I was a little bit worried that maybe you hadn't chosen the right topic, but you really worked hard and made it your own, didn't you?"

Anna beamed.

"Hi, Anna!" said Mr. Hoffman.

Anna turned around, surprised. She hadn't even noticed him standing right next to her, since she'd been so excited to tell Miss Lopez about her project. "Hi, Mr. Hoffman," she said, then she turned back to Miss Lopez. "We have to make sure we make a lot of places for butterflies to lay their eggs. That's important."

Miss Lopez put on her serious face and nodded. "Whoa! We have a long way to go before we have to worry about butterflies laying eggs. Why don't you get started on your project, and we'll see where it takes us?"

"Okay." Anna nodded. Now that she had a topic she truly cared about, she couldn't wait to get to work.

The bell rang, and Anna went to the back of the line, waving at her friends as she walked past them. Anna would have to work super hard on her research and her presentation. She'd help her class make great compost, and Miss Lopez would finally ask her to work in the butterfly garden.

The fun forecast was finally predicting good weather! Even though it was August, Anna felt like she was about to spring into spring.

RAINBOWS ALL THE WAY

The next Wednesday, Anna's mother took the morning off work so she could come see Anna's presentation (and help her carry all her materials). Anna had spent almost all of her spare time the past week collecting everything she would need. A stack of plastic drawer bins with holes cut into the tops and bottoms for air. Lots of cardboard and newspaper, all shredded up. Vegetable scraps from her mom's restaurant. And last but not least, Anna used the money in her piggy bank to buy one thousand red wigglers. They were the best kind of worms for vermicomposting.

Anna had also done something else. Her presentation wasn't just about worms anymore. The more time she spent working on her Curiosity Quest, the more she realized she didn't want to write about only worms. She wanted to write about the question *she* was burning with curiosity to answer. So she'd changed her question. She hoped Miss Lopez wouldn't mind, but even if she did, Anna was ready. Working on the project had already been fun enough.

Anna and her mother had driven to school, even though it was only a couple blocks away.

They parked in the teachers' parking lot and carried all the supplies into Room 13. Finally, the school bell rang, and Anna's classmates followed Miss Lopez politely down the hall. Anna took her seat.

Miss Lopez looked at Anna when she entered the classroom. "Did you get everything set up all right, Anna?"

Anna nodded her head, and that's when the wriggling started in her stomach. It felt like the worms were in her belly instead of in the white plastic bucket on the table. Each day that week five kids from Anna's class had given their presentations. Anna had watched Reed's magic show, Bailey's planetarium show, and Kaya's art lesson. She'd also taken a knot-tying lesson, played a video game that a girl in her class had coded, and watched a pretend cooking show video of how to make a cake that looks like a castle. She got to eat some of the cake too.

Each presentation had been wonderful. And Miss Lopez had smiled, clapped, and given each presenter a special compliment at the end. Anna knew what the wriggly worms in her stomach meant. They were there because she didn't know if Miss Lopez would give her a compliment. What if Miss Lopez was mad that Anna changed her question? What if she told Anna her presentation was no good, right in front of Anna's mom and the whole entire class? What if Anna *never* got picked to work in the butterfly garden?

"Anna?" Miss Lopez said after they finished the Pledge of Allegiance. "Are you ready to begin?"

Anna gulped, stood up, and walked to the

back of the room. She straightened her trifold presentation board, but before she opened it, she shot one nervous glance at her mother, sitting in a big chair next to Miss Lopez's desk. Her mother gave her two thumbs-up. Anna took a deep breath and began.

"Hello, everyone. I am so excited to be here today to talk to you about a very important question."

Anna opened up her trifold poster board so everyone could see the question written out in rainbow bubble letters.

"How can we make our butterfly garden the best butterfly garden it can be?"

Anna's eyes flicked over to Miss Lopez to see what she thought about the change of topic, but Miss Lopez wasn't looking at Anna. She was scribbling something in her notebook.

Anna's worms got even wigglier, but she kept going. There were three main things that had to be considered. First, the plants.

"We will have to plant lots of different kinds of flowers and plants in our garden," Anna told the class. "We'll need milkweed plants, of course, but also violets, snapdragons, and even carrots."

Second, the habitat. Anna told her classmates that it was nice to have shallow pools of water for the butterflies to drink from. Also, the garden needed to be in a really sunny spot.

"Butterflies are cold-blooded, and they can only fly when their wings are warm, so they need a lot of places to spread their wings and bask in the sunshine." Anna held up her brother's monarch butterfly puppet and spread its wings wide to demonstrate.

"Finally," Anna continued, "to make a great butterfly garden, we will have to start with great soil. One thing that helps make soil really great is compost, and today I'm going to get our class started with our very own vermicomposting bin. *Vermicomposting* means using worms to make compost."

While her classmates watched, Anna carefully filled one of the plastic bins with shredded newspaper and cardboard and sprayed them with enough water so that they were damp, but not soaking. Then she buried the chopped-up vegetable scraps in the middle of her pile. She let each student who wanted to come up to the table and add a handful of worms to the bin.

Some kids wrinkled their noses and stayed in their chairs, but a lot of kids couldn't wait to touch the worms.

Bailey giggled as she scooped up a handful of worms and put them in the compost bin. "They feel cold!" she said. "And wet."

Anna nodded. "Worms have to have moist skin in order to breathe," Anna told her. "We'll have to make sure that our compost bin never gets too dried out, or they might die."

"But I don't get it," Reed said as he picked up a handful and held it up high, watching the worms dangle between his fingers. "How do the worms turn all this stuff into compost? Doesn't compost look like dirt?"

"Compost does look like dirt." Anna bit her bottom lip. She wasn't sure what the kids would say when they realized what vermicompost was made out of. "Right now the stuff in our bins looks like paper and vegetables, but the worms living in the com-post bin will eat all of that stuff and then—"

Anna gulped. She snuck another look at Miss Lopez, but she was still writing in her notebook, so Anna tried again. "And then, after the worms eat the food, they will digest it, and then, um, they will put it back in the compost bin."

Anna took a deep breath. *Phew!* She hadn't been sure how she was going to explain it, but she did.

"But how do they put it back in the bin?" a boy from Anna's class asked. "Do they throw up?"

"Aaaah!" a girl screamed. "Is compost made out of worm throw-up? Disgusting!"

Anna felt her cheeks turn pink. Her voice got very tiny. "Compost isn't made out of worm throw-up," she said. "It, um, actually comes out the other end."

There was complete silence in the classroom for a moment. Anna's heart was pounding so hard, it felt like her rib cage was shaking. Then everyone burst into laughter.

"POOP?" Reed screamed. "Compost is made out of worm poop?"

"Technically, it's called *worm castings*," Anna said. "But yes. Compost is worm poop." Anna couldn't believe she'd just said the word *P-O-O-P* out loud in front of her entire class.

"There is no way I'm touching poop!" a kid from the back of the class shouted.

"Does that mean that all of our vegetables will be covered with worm poop?" Kaya asked.

"Only the ones grown with vermicompost," Anna said with a shrug. "But we always wash our vegetables before we eat them anyway."

Anna tried to explain how nutritious vermicompost was for the soil, but everyone was either laughing or pretending to be grossed out. No one was listening anymore.

Miss Lopez stood up. "*¡Silencio, por favor!*"

Everyone quieted down quickly and went back to their seats.

"Anna," Miss Lopez continued. "Was there anything else you wanted to tell us?"

Miss Lopez was not smiling. She held her notebook pressed against her chest.

Anna shook her head. "I'm done," she squeaked.

Miss Lopez nodded her head. Anna's heart  fell into her stomach. Then Miss Lopez burst into a huge smile. "That was excellent, Anna. Our class is certainly lucky to have a student so interested in our butterfly garden. With your help, I'm sure it will be a great success. Would you be willing to work in the garden at recess today?"

Would she? Anna's smiled practically filled the whole room. "I can't wait!" Suddenly, the forecast for fourth grade was rainbows all the way!

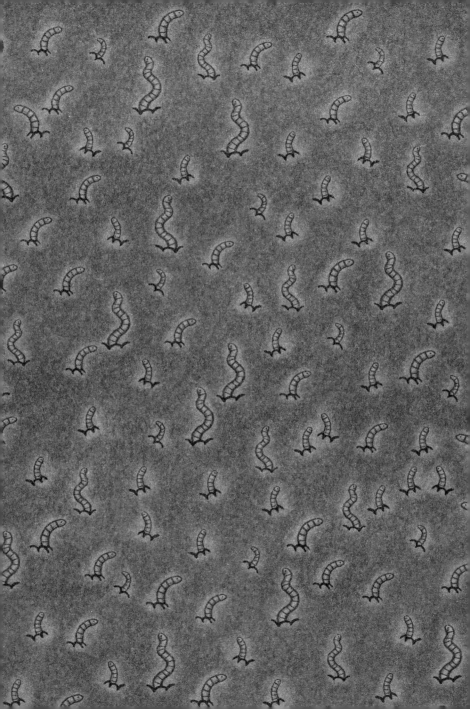

ACTIVITY: **MAKE YOUR OWN SQUIRMY, WORMY GUMMY WORMS!**

What you will need:

1 16-ounce plastic cup

100 adjustable plastic drinking straws with crinkle part fully extended

3-4 rubber bands

1 ½ cups fruit juice (If you have a juicer, you can make your own juice!)

4 tablespoons gelatin

1-3 tablespoons honey (optional)

½ teaspoon vanilla (optional)

Step One: Make the Gummy Mixture

1. Pour the juice into a small saucepan. With the help of a grown-up, heat the juice on

medium heat until the juice is very warm but not boiling.

2. Turn off the heat and slowly sprinkle the gelatin into the juice while whisking it together.

3. Now add the honey and vanilla if you want a sweeter flavor.

Step Two: Make the Worm Mold

1. Bundle all your straws together and fasten them with at least three rubber bands. Make sure all the extendable crinkle parts are facing the same direction.

2. Put the straw bundle into your plastic cup with the extendable crinkle parts toward the bottom of the cup.

3. With the help of a grown-up, pour your liquid gelatin mixture into the straws, making sure

to fill each straw. There will be extra liquid at the bottom of the cup—that's okay.

4. Refrigerate the cup of straws for at least two hours.

5. When the gelatin is set, take the straw bundle out of the cup and remove the excess gelatin from the outside of the straws.

6. Then, taking one straw at a time, gently squeeze the straw together at the point in the middle of the straw, just past the end of the gelatin. Now slide your squeezed fingers in the direction of the bumpy end of the straw and watch your worm squiggle out of the straw.

7. Keep your gummy worms refrigerated in a Ziploc bag. They keep for three days.

Looking for another great book?
Find it
IN THE MIDDLE.

Fun, fantastic books for kids
in the in-be**TWEEN** age.

IntheMiddleBooks.com

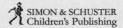